THE MAZE

Sue Graves

RISING★STARS

Rising Stars UK Ltd.
7 Hatchers Mews, Bermondsey Street, London SE1 3GS
www.risingstars-uk.com

nasen
Helping Everyone Achieve
■ ■ ■ **nasen**

NASEN House, 4/5 Amber Business Village, Amber Close,
Amington, Tamworth, Staffordshire B77 4RP

Published 2012

Author: Sue Graves
Series editor: Sasha Morton
Text and logo design: pentacor**big**
Typesetting: Geoff Rayner, Bag of Badgers
Cover design: Lon Chan
Publisher: Gill Budgell
Project Manager: Sasha Morton Creative Project Management
Editorial: Deborah Kespert
Artwork: Colour: Lon Chan / B&W: Paul Loudon

British Library Cataloguing in Publication Data.
A CIP record for this book is available from the British Library.

ISBN: 978-0-85769-610-6

Printed by Craftprint International, Singapore

CHAPTER 1

It was a sunny day and Tom, Sima and Kojo decided to have their lunch in the park. Their office had been hot and stuffy all morning, but outdoors it was much cooler.

Tom, Sima and Kojo worked at Dangerous Games, a computer games company. Sima designed the games and Kojo programmed them. Tom's job was to test the games to check that they were satisfying to play and that they were good value for the customer. They all loved their jobs and they were best mates, too.

Sima, Tom and Kojo found a shady tree in the park and sat down beneath it. Sima handed out some sandwiches, fruit and drinks and everyone tucked in. After a while, Kojo pulled out a paperback from his pocket and began to read.

"What's your book about, Kojo?" asked Sima, peering over his shoulder.

"It's all about Greek legends," said Kojo. "It's really interesting."

"That reminds me of stuff we had to learn in school," snorted Tom. "I thought it was boring. Even the teachers were boring!"

"Well, this isn't boring at all. In fact, I'm learning loads," said Kojo. "This part is about the weird mazes or labyrinths that the Greeks made. It says here that the first one they built was to imprison the Minotaur."

"What was the Minotaur?" asked Sima, biting into an apple.

"It was a man-eating monster," explained Kojo. "Apparently, it was half man and half bull."

"That's given me an idea," said Sima. She pulled a notebook and pencil out of her bag and started to scribble some notes.

"Sima, it's lunchtime," moaned Tom, stretching out on the grass and closing his eyes against the hot sun. "Don't you ever take a break from work?"

"Yes, of course I do," said Sima. "But listen, I've got this great idea for a new game. The players have to take turns to navigate their way through a maze, or labyrinth. They will carry a special route finder to lead them to the middle, where the monster's lair is. The player then uses a button on the route finder to activate a laser and destroy the monster. Simple!"

"How will you know who the winning player is?" asked Kojo.

"The winner will be the one who completes the task the fastest," said Sima. "To make it more difficult, I'll add traps and obstacles in the labyrinth. We haven't done a strategy game like this for ages. It could be amazing."

Tom yawned and stretched lazily. He looked at his watch and then jumped up. "Oh no, look at the time, guys. We'd better get back to the office fast or the boss will have turned into a man-eating monster!"

CHAPTER 2

For the next few days, Sima researched ideas for the new game. She designed an amazing labyrinth with lots of traps and obstacles. She finally showed the boys her ideas when they stopped for a coffee break.

"What do you think?" she asked them.

"It's really good," said Tom. "I especially like the design for the route finder. That's cool."

"Yeah," agreed Kojo, "the gadget's the best bit of all."

Sima grinned. "I knew that would appeal to you," she said. "You two always like games that have extra gadgets in them."

Kojo looked carefully at the designs. "These look very straightforward," he said. "I'll have these programmed in a day or so."

Soon, Kojo had programmed the game. He handed it to Tom for testing.

"I've got an idea. Let's test it for real," suggested Kojo. "I'd love to try out the route finder."

"You know, I'd like to try this one for real, too," admitted Sima. "I'd love to see how well it works. It would be good fun to see which one of us can destroy the monster in the quickest time, too."

"OK," said Tom. "But as only one player can enter the game at a time, we need to decide who's going first."

They all wrote their names on pieces of paper and put the notes into a bag. Tom shook the bag hard.

"Pull out a name, Kojo," he said.

Kojo shut his eyes and put his hand into the bag. He pulled out a slip of paper and read the name on it. It was Sima. Kojo was disappointed.

"So you're going first, Sima," said Tom. He handed her the route finder. "Have fun but be careful. Kojo and I will be able to follow your progress on screen. But we won't be able to communicate with you, so try not to scare us by doing anything dangerous."

Kojo loaded the game onto the computer. "Remember the usual rules apply," he said. "However, in this case you must touch the screen alone, Sima, to enter the game. The game is only over when you hear the words 'Game Over'. OK?"

"OK," said Sima. She looked nervous. "It's a bit scary going into a game on my own."

"You'll be fine," said Tom grinning. "Just don't get eaten by the Minotaur. That would wreck the game for the rest of us."

"You're not funny, you know," said Sima.

She touched the screen. A bright light flashed and she shut her eyes tight.

CHAPTER 3

The bright light faded and Sima opened her eyes.
She was standing in hot sunshine at the opening
of a huge labyrinth. She switched on the route
finder and, pointing it towards the labyrinth,
walked slowly inside.

The labyrinth was hot and stuffy and strangely quiet. She looked hard for any traps or obstacles, and at first, everything seemed OK. Then suddenly, the ground gave way and a huge crack opened up beneath her feet. Quickly, she jumped over the gap, but she lost her footing and slid back. As she fell, she stretched out and grabbed a root sticking out of the crack. Then, using all her strength, she scrambled to safety.

She sat on the ground to catch her breath and stared down into the gaping hole. She watched as it slowly faded and then disappeared. Brushing dirt off her clothes, Sima stood up and walked further into the maze.

PHEW. THAT WAS A NARROW ESCAPE.

"She's doing brilliantly," said Kojo as they watched her on the screen. "She's avoided the hole, but I hope she's spotted those spikes above her head."

Sima walked right under the spikes but looked up just in time as they hurtled down towards her. Quickly, she flattened herself against the side of the labyrinth. The spikes whistled past her, missing her by inches and embedding themselves in the ground. Sima breathed a sigh of relief and then watched as the spikes faded away.

"Wow! That was close," gasped Tom.

47:00

Just then, there was a loud click and the screen went blank. The boys heard the words 'Game Over'.

"That was quick," said Kojo, looking puzzled. "I didn't think she was anywhere near the middle of the labyrinth."

"Me, neither," said Tom.

They waited and waited for Sima to appear in the office. But nothing happened.

"This isn't right," said Kojo, looking worried. "She should be back here by now. It's nearly 10 minutes since we heard the 'Game Over' voice. What shall we do?"

"Re-open the game, quickly!" cried Tom. He was starting to realise that something had gone badly wrong.

Kojo tried to re-open the game but nothing happened.

Tom paced up and down. He was really worried.

"There's only one thing to do," he said after a few minutes. "I'll reload the game onto my computer. I may be able to enter the game world in a new session. If I'm lucky, I might be able to cross over into Sima's game and bring her back out with me."

"But you won't have the route finder," said Kojo. "There's only one handset and Sima has it."

Tom thought for a few seconds. He pulled out his mobile phone. "I'll upload the plan of the labyrinth on this," he said. "At least it will help me to get my bearings if nothing else."

He uploaded the plan from Sima's game design and then touched the screen. A bright light flashed and he shut his eyes tight.

CHAPTER 4

The bright light faded and Tom found himself inside the labyrinth. The obstacles and traps came thick and fast. First, he had to sidestep a snakepit. The snakes hissed and reared out of the pit to try and bite him.

THIS IS REALLY SCARY!

59:00

Next, he heard a loud bubbling sound and a huge fountain of boiling oil gushed out of the ground. Tom flattened himself against the side of the labyrinth. The boiling oil just missed him.

Then, huge spiders crawled out of cracks in the ground. The spiders had long fangs that dripped with poison. Tom picked up handfuls of small rocks and threw them at the spiders. He managed to hit some, but the others got away.

Tom walked on through the labyrinth, but it got hotter and hotter, and he felt himself becoming weaker and weaker. His mouth was dry and his throat was burning with thirst.

I'VE GOT TO KEEP GOING. I'VE GOT TO FIND SIMA.

He looked down at his phone. The plan of the labyrinth was fading fast. He turned the phone off and on again, but it was no good. The battery was completely dead.

39:00

Tom walked on and on until he came to a fork in the maze.

"Which way do I go now?" he muttered. He looked carefully at the two paths that opened up before him. Then he looked at the ground. On one of the paths there was a faint outline of a footprint.

"It must be Sima's footprint," he said. He looked all around and called her name. But there was no reply.

CHAPTER 5

Tom looked at his watch. The game time was starting to run out. He ran along the path and down a long, steep slope. After a few minutes, the slope opened up into a clearing. In the corner, there was a huge bed of straw. Nearby was a deep pit of fire. Flames and hot ash shot up out of the pit. Tom felt scared. Not only was he in the centre of the labyrinth, he was in the heart of the monster's lair!

"Tom, Tom!" yelled a voice. He looked up and saw Sima. She was trapped in a large cage. It was held above the ground by a thick rope hanging from a rock. She looked terrified.

I'M COMING.

Just then, a dark shadow fell over
Tom. He spun round and, to his horror,
saw a huge monster behind him. It was
the Minotaur – half man and half bull.
The Minotaur had huge, powerful jaws
and long pointed horns. With a roar of
anger, it turned on Tom. Sima screamed as
it pinned him to the ground. Tom kicked out
at the animal and rolled away. He scrambled
to his feet and ran behind some rocks. But the
monster had seen where Tom had hidden and
was heading straight for him.

"Oh no," groaned Tom, "I think this really is
'Game Over' for me."

He looked up at the sky. The sun was beating down
hard and, suddenly, Tom had a great idea.

18:00

33

Tom pulled out his phone and directed the screen so that it caught the sun's rays. Very slowly, he rotated the screen so that the rays flashed into the beast's eyes and blinded it. The monster bellowed in pain and fell backwards straight into the pit of fire.

OOH, NASTY!
I BET THAT
HURT.

35

Then, Tom ran over to the rope that was holding Sima's cage above the ground. He tugged at the rope hard but it would not budge.

He looked around on the ground for something to help and spotted a long piece of wood. He quickly grabbed it. Next, he gathered up some straw from the monster's bedding and wound it round the end of the wood to make a torch. Covering his face from the heat, he carefully lowered the torch into the fire until the straw caught light.

Tom held the flame to the rope. The rope burnt through and the cage crashed to the ground.
The impact of the crash forced the door of the cage to slam open.

Sima leapt free as a bright light flashed. They shut their eyes tightly as they heard the words 'Game Over'.

CHAPTER 6

The bright light faded and they opened their eyes. Tom and Sima were safely back in the office. They could see Kojo standing at Tom's computer. He was desperately trying to activate the screen. He didn't know that Tom and Sima were behind him.

"Hey! Get your hands off my computer!" called Tom.

Kojo spun round at the sound of Tom's voice.

Tom grinned at him. "That scared you! You look as if you've seen a ghost."

"Thank goodness you're safe," said Kojo. "I've been so worried. The screen went blank in your game in exactly the same place that it did with Sima's. I thought I'd lost both of you."

"No worries!" said Tom, patting Kojo on the back. "We're back and that's all that matters."

"Tom's my hero, though," grinned Sima. "You should have seen him defeat the Minotaur! He was incredibly brave."

"I wish I could have seen it," sighed Kojo. "I can't believe the game failed like that."

Then Tom looked serious. "This game definitely has way too many problems right now. You need to look at your programming more carefully, Kojo."

"I know," said Kojo. "I feel awful for putting you both at risk."

Tom looked at his watch. It was almost nine o'clock. "It's getting late," he said. "But I suggest you stay in the office and do some overtime, Kojo, until you've got the game right. There are some sandwiches left over from lunchtime. They should keep you going."

Kojo looked at the dry, curled-up sandwiches and sighed. "So what are you and Sima going to do?"

"We're going out for dinner," said Tom. "I think we deserve it."

"Where are you going to eat?" asked Kojo taking a bite out of his stale sandwich and chewing it miserably.

"I'm really starving. Defeating a legendary monster has given me an appetite," said Tom. "I think I'll have one of the Monster Meals at Frankie's Café. What about you, Sima?"

"Ooh yes, a Monster Meal sounds perfect," said Sima, and they left the office laughing loudly.

GLOSSARY OF TERMS

bearing(s) to get your bearings means to find out where you are and where other things are

clearing an area where there are no trees or bushes

gadget(s) a small tool or piece of equipment that does something useful

labyrinth a maze

lair an animal's den

legend(s) an old story about events from the past that isn't usually true

navigate to find and follow a path in a particular direction

obstacle a thing that blocks the way

pace(d) to walk around a small area continuously because you are worried

paperback a book with a cover made of thick paper

rotate(d) to move in a circle around a fixed point

scramble(d) to climb using your feet and hands

scribble untidy writing

sidestep to step quickly to the side

stuffy airless

torch a piece of wood with a flame at one end to give light

Quiz

1 What paperback was Kojo reading?

2 What was the name of the man-eating monster in the labyrinth?

3 Which gadget did Sima design for the game?

4 Name one of the obstacles Sima had to overcome in the labyrinth.

5 Name one obstacle that Tom had to overcome when he entered the labyrinth.

6 What made Tom decide to choose a particular path at the fork in the labyrinth?

7 Where did the slope lead?

8 Where was Sima?

9 How did Tom blind the monster?

10 What happened to the monster?

About the Author

Sue Graves has taught for thirty years in Cheshire schools. She has been writing for more than ten years and has written well over a hundred books for children and young adults.

"Nearly everyone loves computer games. They are popular with all age groups — especially young adults. But I've often thought it would be amazing to play a computer game for real. To be in on the action would be the best experience ever! That's why I wrote these stories. I hope you enjoy reading them as much as I've enjoyed writing them for you."

ANSWERS TO QUIZ

1   A book about Greek legends

2   The Minotaur

3   A route finder

4   A hole in the ground or spikes falling on her

5   A snakepit, boiling oil or huge spiders

6   He saw a footprint on the ground

7   To a clearing

8   In a cage

9   Using the screen on his mobile phone, he reflected the sun's rays into the monster's eyes

10 The monster fell into the pit of fire